The Space Person

Catherine Kuo

Timber Ghost Press

The Space Person

Published by Timber Ghost Press

Printed in the United States of America

Edited by: Beverly Bernard

Cover Art and Design by: Wes (SenatorGreaves) Greaves

https://www.senatorgreaves.com

Interior Design: Timber Ghost Press

Print ISBN: 979-8-9883040-9-8

www.TimberGhostPress.com

Contents

Dedicated to my mother and stepfather.

The Space Person

"Run the scans again."

"I ran it three times already, Cap, it's not a glitch," said First Officer Jasmine Donnelly. She turned and grinned. "It's the real deal."

Captain Annie Chou stroked her chin, her dark eyes reflecting the light from the holo-displays, and the corner of her mouth twitching upward into a smile. She let out a bark of laughter and slapped Donnelly on the back.

"Yes. Yes! This is it! This could give us enough fuel to last the next hundred years, at least! We bring this back, the entire world's gonna go nuts."

"The company's gonna go nuts when they find out we crossed into uncharted space," Donnelly laughed.

"Whatever. No risk, no reward. With the kind of profit this will bring in, they'll forgive us. I'm going to get the mining crew up to speed. Set a course and send a report to HQ."

"You got it, Cap."

Chou's thick boots tapped a heavy litany on the cold, metal floor of the ship's winding corridors as she strode toward the crew's quarters. Her ship, the Shiro Oni, emitted its usual creaks and purrs, and she ran her fingers along its imperfect but clean walls. Chou's chief engineer, Stella Kidane, would no doubt be holed up in her room, reading some boring manuscript with a lot of math and imaginary numbers in it.

"Stella, it's me," she called, rapping her knuckles three times on the door. It slid open to reveal a lean, muscular woman in a gray t-shirt and cargo pants, her afro pulled back into a puff ponytail.

"Cap," said Kidane, her voice deep and mellow.

"We got ourselves a rock with fuel," said Chou, smiling, unable to contain her excitement. "This could be the big one. Get your team ready to dig. We'll be landing in about four hours, and I want to get some samples ASAP."

"We'll be ready," said Kidane without any change in inflection.

As soon as Chou bounced back down the hallway, Kidane slipped back into her room. Her manuscript would have to wait. It would likely take her the full four hours to wrangle the rest of her team and get them up to speed.

She first sought out Charlie Vasquez, whose sole title was engineer despite his insistence on inserting himself into every other process taking place aboard the ship. But he was a people person by nature, and his penchant for gossip sometimes saved Kidane the trouble of dispersing news to the rest of the team. She then found the lead geologist, Sanjay Garcia, who was both relieved they could finally begin work and annoyed she had interrupted him in the middle of sending one of his precious transmissions to his husband back on Mars.

When they had all assembled in the common area, Kidane reminded them of their designated tasks and protocol before sending them on their way in teams to prepare for the dig. The operation was a fairly simple one, but they had been sedentary for the past few months while the Shiro Oni floated through the galaxy, and there was no harm in a refresher course, especially given how eager Captain Chou was about the moon they'd found.

The engineers completed their final checks of the machinery and equipment just as Chou's announcement came over the intercom, ordering everyone to strap in for landing.

"Don't you think you're leaning a little too hard on the throttle?" said Vasquez, who had somehow managed to worm his way on deck and sit right behind First Officer Donnelly.

"Dammit, Charlie, I know how to pilot the ship. I doubt you've even driven a dune buggy before. How about you don't tell me how to do my job, and I won't tell you how to do yours."

"I'm just saying, Jasmine, it feels like—"

"If you don't shut the hell up right now—"

"Jasmine, Vasquez, stow it," said Chou, gazing intently at the dusty, cement-white surface of the moon.

Down in the loading bay, Kidane and Garcia stood by as the ship thunked and rumbled through the atmosphere, the chains holding down the equipment clanking and rattling like a chorus of jingle bells.

"How long do you think the dig'll take?" asked Garcia, ruffling his curly hair.

"Not more than a week or two at most, probably," said Kidane. "Annie said she might want to try mapping out the rest of the system though."

"Are you kidding me? We came out here to look for fuel, not another barren planet to squat on. I just want to go home. Shit, I hope I can make it back for Zulis's birthday. She's turning six," he grumbled.

To Kidane's relief, their conversation came to an abrupt halt as the ship completed its turbulent landing. Within ten minutes, the rest of her team suited up and met them on the loading dock to drag the dig equipment out onto the surface. The gravity of the moon was manageable, and they were able to get everything set up about a kilometer from the ship within a few hours.

Chou and Donnelly had insisted the moon was a veritable treasure trove, but most of the crew agreed it didn't look any more unique than the other moons and asteroids they had inspected over the years. Perhaps less full of craters, but it lacked any notable topographical features. Just a white, cloudy marble circling a candy-striped gas giant, much like how Earth's moon used to look before humans fled there, before the second apocalypse that drove the survivors to Mars.

They spent the next few days making shallow, experimental drills and analyzing the samples acquired at various depths. Everything proceeded according to plan, though perhaps too much so for most of the mining crew, whose only source of entertainment was watching the drill spin slowly against a featureless, white backdrop.

"Doesn't this place give off weird vibes though?" said Jean Wilson, one of the engineers. They had just finished their fourth day on the job and had emerged from the mildly unpleasant decontamination chamber.

"You say that about every rock we land on," laughed Vasquez, stepping out of his suit.

"Yeah, but I've been having this odd recurring dream ever since we landed."

"What about?"

"Um, well, it's like I'm in a dark void, but it kind of feels heavy? The darkness, I mean. And I can hear relaxing music, or what's supposed to sound relaxing, but I don't feel relaxed at all. I feel claustrophobic. And then I see a thing that looks almost like a person. It's got a long head, long legs, and long arms, and it's got space inside it. Or it's made of space? I can see stars and galaxies and planets moving in it, and it just stands there looking at me."

"Have you been taking your meds, Jean?" said Vasquez, pulling on his boots with a grin.

"Yes, and this has nothing to do with that." Wilson frowned. "And it's the same every night. Sets my teeth on edge. I don't know why. It's the music, I think."

"Right. Sure. Do me a favor and see your therapist when we get home."

"I was going to, but this has nothing to do with that," Wilson mumbled as they headed to the cafeteria.

They met their colleague, Yumi Costa, coming out of the locker room, and she joined them on their journey to dinner.

"You okay, Yumi?" said Vasquez. "You keep flexing your fingers. Did you hurt yourself working the drill?"

"Huh? Oh. No, nothing happened with the drill. I don't know, I just feel kind of stiff, but like all over?"

"Pretty sure you're too young for arthritis." Vasquez chuckled, but Costa ignored his poor attempt at humor.

"Or like I've had too much caffeine. You know the feeling?"

"Lay off the coffee then."

"Yeah, maybe."

"Just don't fall into the drill. Jasmine would bring you back to life just to kill you for inconveniencing her."

"Hmm," said Costa, though she wasn't listening, too preoccupied with staring at her long, slim fingers as if she didn't recognize them.

They entered the cafeteria and took their usual places at the engineers' table. Meals were only served during designated hours of the day, which meant everyone ate around the same time, but the cafeteria always ended up segregated among the engineers, geologists, and ship's crew. Chou and Donnelly occupied a single table, deemed the officers' table by unspoken agreement among the rest, and the only other exception was Kidane, who liked to sit alone in the corner with her manuscripts for company. She was not unsociable, nor did her engineers particularly fear or dislike her, they simply chose to leave her alone out of respect.

Garcia was the lead geologist, but he didn't consider himself of equal rank to Kidane or the ship's officers. He liked to sit with the rest of his team, even if they were tired of him showing them pictures of his daughter. Today, however, Chou and Donnelly had invited him to their table to discuss his team's progress in analyzing their current samples.

"To cut to the chase, the results are looking good," he explained. "Just a couple more days and I think we'll have a good sample size to bring back to Mars."

"Perfect," said Chou, beaming. "Well done, Sanjay."

"And you said we wouldn't find anything," Donnelly teased.

"That's because we haven't found anything in years. You can't blame me for losing hope," said Garcia, shaking his head.

"Well, we've got hope now," said Chou. "Not just us, but everyone back home."

"Speaking of back home, we're going back home after the dig's finished, right?" said Garcia, raising his eyebrows. Chou and Donnelly suddenly found other parts of the cafeteria extremely interesting.

"Ah, well, you know, when you've hit the jackpot, you might as well take a chance at doubling it, right?" said Chou.

"When you hit the jackpot, you cash out," said Garcia, glaring at her.

"Oh, come on, Sanjay. Think about what it could mean for us if we find a habitable planet! Don't you want a better life for your family?"

"Annie, we've worked together long enough that I know you care more about money than people," Garcia snorted.

"Well, I care about people," interjected Donnelly, leaning forward. "We could really make a difference here. Seriously. This moon is proof that there's hope out there. We just have to be persistent. When it comes to saving humanity, we have to tough out the minor inconveniences."

"Minor inconveniences being my daughter's birthday?"

"Everyone on this ship's made sacrifices to be here," she continued. "But they're doing it because this work means something, and it's something more than just money."

Chou nodded solemnly, and Garcia scoffed at her mock sincerity. He stood up, lunch tray in one hand. "This isn't in my contract, Annie."

She waved away his parting shot. Then, to Donnelly's dismay, Vasquez slid into Garcia's empty seat.

"Are we really going to explore the system after this?"

"Buzz off, Vasquez, it's rude to eavesdrop," said Donnelly.

"Speaking of eavesdropping, I heard Kealani and Alexandr might have a thing going on. Do you know if that's true?"

"What?" Donnelly spluttered. Chou had already tuned them out, sipping her coffee with a faraway look in her eyes. "Where the hell did that come from? And no, Alexandr's got a girlfriend back on Mars."

"Sure, but they're always glued at the hip. There's got to be something."

"Yeah, something like they're just really good friends and coworkers. Stop trying to stir up drama, Charlie," said Donnelly, flipping her long cornrow braids into his face. "It may be boring waiting for you and the others to finish playing with rocks, but I'm not that bored. Though it might be kind of entertaining if a moon beast appeared and ate you up."

"Poor Sanjay, does no one read his reports except me and the captain? Otherwise, you'd know that not even a single strand of bacteria inhabits this place, much less a moon beast," Vasquez chortled.

"It's about time we get back to work," said Chou, standing up before Donnelly could throw a haymaker at Vasquez's smug face.

The following days passed by without incident, though Wilson and Costa continued to complain of strange dreams and restlessness. When Vasquez reported their symptoms to Kidane, she chalked it up to the change in environment, but her theory began to waver at the end of the week when during dinner, a sudden clatter penetrated the dull hum of conversation in the cafeteria and snapped her out of the world of p values and hypotheses. All eyes turned toward Wilson, who hastily bent down to pick up the tray he had dropped, hands shaking. Kidane rose and reached him in a few long strides.

"You okay?" she asked, scooping slop back onto the plastic tray with her bare hands.

"Yeah, just a little jittery, that's all," he said breathily, as if he had just returned from a jog.

"That doesn't sound okay to me. You're supposed to be operating heavy machinery tomorrow. Maybe you should rest. Meyer can cover for you."

"No, no, I'll be fine, I promise. I had strange dreams last night, so I didn't sleep well, but I'll sleep better tonight."

"Okay, but if you still don't feel well tomorrow, I'm not having you out there."

"Roger that," he said, smiling weakly.

A few meters over, Vasquez joined Chou and Donnelly at their table once again. Donnelly's face crinkled with disgust.

"What's up with Jean?" he said in a low voice.

"You know, sometimes humans do things like accidentally drop stuff? Not sure if you were aware?" Donnelly sneered.

"Yeah, but I was talking to Yumi a few minutes ago, and she was all twitchy too. She's been like that since we started the dig."

"So?"

"So, she's supposed to be working the drill, right? What if she slips and gets a leg ripped to shreds?"

Donnelly shot Chou an exasperated look, but the captain didn't notice, preoccupied with studying Wilson.

"Keep an eye on them," said Chou. "Everyone passed their health checks before they got on board, so there's no reason for it to be anything serious. But if people are unwell, I don't want anyone getting hurt out there. If they start to feel worse, Jasmine, take them down to med bay."

Chou scarfed down the rest of her nutritional sludge and excused herself, leaving Donnelly stranded with Vasquez.

"I can come too. I had some medical training while I was in the milita—"

"That will be completely unnecessary, Charlie," Donnelly growled. "I have plenty of experience."

Their bickering followed Chou all the way out of the cafeteria until the heavy metal doors hissed shut behind her. She made her way up to the bridge and plopped into the chair in front of the communications panel.

"New transmission to Kami Resources, Inc., New Johannesburg, Mars, R-six-zero-zero-nine-eight-two-six-one-five-seven."

"Recording," said the computer.

"Drills and analyses are being carried out as planned, and we should be able to complete sample collection in the next few days. Given that this is the first time a ship from the African Union has entered this system, I would like to request direct written correspondence with Mr. Eze to ask for permission to continue exploration in case there are any habitable planetary bodies or bodies with an abundance of natural resources. End recording."

"Recording complete."

"Send transmission," said Chou.

"Transmission sent."

"What do you mean we're investigating the rest of the system?"

Chou turned to face a fuming Garcia, his hands planted firmly on his hips.

"Sanjay, I didn't hear you come in. Did you need something?" she said, smoothly.

"Yeah, an explanation," he countered. "We did what we came to do. We got the samples, we're done. And now you want us to be out here for another who-knows-how-many months to play space explorer? I didn't sign up for that."

"This is a space-exploration ship, Sanjay," said Chou, leaning back in her seat and crossing her legs. "It always has been. And the purpose of space-exploration ships is to look for ways to sustain humanity. None of us are doing this for fun. It's like Jasmine said: we're doing it for the sake of the people back on Mars. Your husband, your daughter. How many more years can we last, do you think? Certainly, we've lived there longer than our ancestors did on the moon, but Mars can't support us forever. It barely does as it is. So, yes, I understand your frustration. We all want to go home, but this is important. I'm sorry. You'll get paid for the extra time."

"I don't want the money. I want to go home," he said, throwing his hands up. "What can I say to convince you?"

"I've made my decision. It's up to the company now. As soon as we get the go-ahead, we'll set a course to tour as much of the system as we can, fuel permitting. That's final. Now, what did you want to see me about?"

Garcia huffed loudly but couldn't come up with any new arguments. There was nothing he could do if the only two people who could pilot the ship had no intention of turning it around.

"Forget it," he said. Shooting her one last disapproving glare, he stormed out of the room, but not before almost running into Donnelly on her way in.

"Did you break the news to him?" asked Donnelly after the bridge doors had closed.

"Yeah, he didn't take it well."

Donnelly snorted. "He'll just have to deal with it. Anything from the company?"

"Just sent off the ask, though I doubt they'll say no at this point. Think about it, Jasmine. Can you imagine if we found an actual habitable planet? We'd be rich. Famous. The saviors of humanity!"

"I don't really need to be famous or anything, but it'd be nice to get off Mars," Donnelly mused. "And to be honest, I don't think it'll support us for much longer. We're in bad shape. People just don't want to admit it, least of all the politicians."

Chou rolled her eyes. "Don't get me started. I don't care what they do, as long as we get paid."

The bridge doors slid open again but instead of Garcia, Kealani Halabi, one of the geologists, shuffled in.

"Halabi, do you need something?" said Chou, hastily.

"Um, I was hoping to speak to Jasmine?"

"I'm listening," said Donnelly, leaning against the communications panel.

Halabi's eyes darted between them, but neither seemed inclined to provide her with the luxury of one-on-one privacy.

"You're the ship's medical officer too, right?" said Halabi.

"Only if it's really necessary. Why?"

"Can you check on Alexandr? He hasn't been feeling well since the dig."

Donnelly sighed. "He's probably just tired. Everyone passed their health checks before we left."

"Can you just take a look, please?" said Halabi, fidgeting. "I thought it was a cold at first, so I gave him some spray and t-orange, but that's not it."

"Fine," Donnelly grumbled. "Where is he?"

"He's in med bay."

Donnelly glanced at Chou, and the captain nodded. Suppressing another sigh, she followed Halabi out. When they arrived at the med bay, they found Alexandr Chocaj and Jean Wilson sitting on adjacent beds, talking quietly. Hands clutched together, Wilson kicked his feet absentmindedly while Chocaj's left leg jittered up and down.

The med bay had been constructed without windows in order to give the patients as much privacy as possible, but as a result, it gave the impression of a spacious solitary-confinement cell. On the left stood a cold, metallic examination table as well as medicine cabinets filled with various implements, first-aid supplies, and the few essential drugs they could afford. Several metal-framed beds lined the far wall, each with a sheer plastic curtain that, again, was meant for privacy but evoked no sense of comfort whatsoever. The mattresses were as thick as the thinnest futon, and a starchy, threadbare sheet lay across each one.

"What're you doing here, Jean?" said Donnelly as she went over to the medicine cabinet and took out a pair of synthetic gloves.

"Not feeling too great, Jasmine," he stammered.

"I'll take a look at you after Alexandr." She beckoned Chocaj over to the examination table. "And what've you got going on?"

"He's been really restless lately," said Halabi, hovering next to him. "Pacing around his cabin all day, sitting down and standing up a lot when he's awake."

"Alexandr is a big boy. He can speak for himself," said Donnelly. "Alexandr, is that true?"

"Yeah, I mean, well, I guess. I haven't really noticed, but Kealani says that's what I've been doing," said Chocaj. He hadn't stopped jiggling his leg, and Donnelly narrowed her eyes at it, as if she could intimidate it into stopping. "I sleep fine though."

"It's probably just a case of space shock," said Donnelly, fishing around in one of the cabinet drawers. "You were out there for a long time. It's normal. The change in gravity, the light, the ground beneath your feet. It's disorienting, but you'll be fine after you're on the ship for the next couple of weeks. In the meantime, I'll give you some sedatives. And make sure you report this to Sanjay since he's your supervisor."

She handed him a cup containing three red-and-black pills and ushered him and Halabi out of the med bay before turning to Wilson.

"What's up, Jean?"

Wilson squeezed his hands tighter.

"Well, I've been having this recurring dream..."

"About the space person or whatever? Charlie told me," she said, rolling her eyes. "Have you been taking your meds—"

"Every time I wake up," Wilson continued, as if she weren't there, "I feel like this... this suit. This suit of skin and organs and muscle is too tight. It feels like I can't breathe right, but I have no trouble inhaling and exhaling fully. It's been like this for the past week now, and I've tried eating more, eating less, sleeping more, and sleeping less, and none of it has made a difference. It feels like I'm in a straitjacket."

Donnelly frowned.

"Jean," she said, slowly, as if to a small child, "are you taking your meds?"

"Dammit, yes! I'm taking my meds! I haven't once stopped taking my meds, I swear," Wilson shouted, then recoiled, startled by his own outburst. Donnelly sighed and rubbed her forehead.

"Look, Jean, if you're taking your meds like you said, then it's probably the same thing I told Alexandr. Being out there for so long, being away from home for so long, it can stress people out. It's nothing serious. I'll give you a sedative to take now and a sleeping pill for tonight. If it helps, I'll give you another sleeping pill tomorrow. The dig's almost done, and then you don't need to do anything else for the remainder of the trip, so just rest in your room and you'll be fine."

"Okay," he said, though he didn't look convinced. He swallowed the sedative and shuffled out, shoulders hunched.

Donnelly audio recorded the required medical reports, not bothering to hide her skepticism in her phrasing, and returned to the bridge.

"Chocaj okay?" said Chou, lazily swiveling her chair around.

"He's fine. Just a case of space shock. Jean too."

"Wilson? He's still not feeling good?" Chou frowned.

"To be honest, I bet he's off his meds. He was saying some really weird shit."

"Weird like how?"

Donnelly waved off Chou's concern. "He said something about a space person. Being in the dark? I don't know. It was a strange dream, sure, but nothing to get shook up about. He practically yelled at me at one point."

"That's not like him at all," said Chou, pensively. "He's never behaved that way with any of us in the last year since he joined, and Stella's never said anything but good things about him. His psych test checked out too."

"I don't know, Cap, but I wouldn't worry about it. He probably just needs to rest. If he does get snippy with me again though, I'll put him in his place."

Chou didn't say anything for a moment, one finger placed contemplatively on her lips.

"Off the record..." she said, slowly. "Could you go check his cabin to see if he's taking his meds?"

Donnelly raised an eyebrow. "Seriously? I'm pretty sure you wrote the policy on the safeguarding of personal privacy on the ship."

"Once the company approves further exploration of the system, we're gonna be out here for a few more weeks. I don't want him causing us any trouble, least of all making us turn this ship around midway and hop back to Mars."

"Nothing stands between you and the hustle, does it?" Donnelly smiled. Chou shot a cheesy finger gun at her and winked.

"I'll call him up tomorrow to have a chat," said Chou. "You can check then."

"Roger that, Cap."

The next day, Wilson arrived on the bridge looking no less frazzled than he had the previous day. When questioned about whether he had taken the sedative, he responded in the affirmative but said it didn't help. Donnelly left him to describe his strange dreams to Chou and headed to his cabin. The captain had given her the skeleton code for all the crew cabins in case of emergency, and Wilson's door opened to her obediently.

All of the cabins had the same layout: a small, sparsely furnished living room, a bedroom through a door to the right, and the bathroom on the left. Chou was particularly pleased with the private toilets and shower units. Rather than having the gunmetal sheen characteristic of the rest of the ship, the sink, vanity, floor tiles, and shower were a classy porcelain white. By contrast, the living rooms were all a drab brown and contained a single muddy-orange couch and a metal coffee table. Wood was more valuable than diamonds, and the best most people could do was paint the floor and walls a flat shade of brown to mimic their tree of choice. The bedroom was much the same, though at least the cabin mattresses were thicker than those in the med bay.

The first thing Donnelly noticed when she walked into Wilson's cabin was the row of pill bottles lined up neatly on the coffee table. A transparent pill minder sat in front of the bottles, and the boxes corresponding to the days of the week that had already passed were dutifully empty. She gave the inside of the trash can a cursory glance, but her gaze unearthed no pills.

When she investigated the bedroom, she found a tablet journal sitting on Wilson's nightstand. She activated it and a list of entries popped up without asking her for a passcode. Donnelly selected the most recent, and Wilson's soft voice filled the room.

"Every night, I see that space man, woman, person, whatever it is, just standing there. Swaying back and forth, staring at me without eyes, and I wish it would go away. It's not hostile, it's not friendly, it's just… it. It just exists, and it exists to stare at me. I almost want to strangle it."

Donnelly switched the journal off.

On her way back up to the bridge, she ran into Yumi Costa, who stopped Donnelly with a shaky hand.

"Ms. Donnelly, I'm sorry, but could I possibly schedule a time to meet with you in med bay? I, um, I haven't been feeling too good."

Donnelly didn't bother to try and hide the displeasure that sprang onto her face. "Did Alexandr or Jean suggest this to you?"

"What? No?" said Costa, eyebrows turned up in confusion and slight hurt. "I just thought since you're the medical officer…"

"I'm the first officer, and I happen to be a certified paramedic, but that doesn't make me a doctor. Just tell me what's wrong. You don't need to make an appointment."

"It's... fine. Never mind," she said, eyes welling up as she pushed past Donnelly.

"Hey, hey," said Donnelly, grabbing Costa's arm. "Look, I'm sorry, I just have some things on my mind. Say what you were going to say."

"Well," said Costa, looking at the ground. "I guess I've been feeling really anxious lately. But only physically. Like my body's tense and shaky for no reason, but then I get worried about it and then I'm anxious in my head too. Does that make sense?"

"Not really, but go on."

"My joints are tight," Costa continued, flexing her fingers. "You know when you're sitting in the same position for a long time and then you have to stretch out your muscles? Except when I stretch, the tight feeling doesn't go away. I stopped drinking coffee, I've been doing yoga, but nothing's changed. And this recurring dream I've been having isn't helping."

"Recurring dream?" said Donnelly, eyes narrowing. Costa nodded.

"It started halfway through the dig, and it's been coming back every night. I'm in the dark, can't see a floor, walls, ceiling, anything. And there's this, I don't know how to describe it, a person? But not actually. It's not shaped like a human being, but it's got a long head and arms and legs. It's not solid though. When I look at it, it's like I'm looking through a window. And on the other side of the window is the galaxy, the universe."

"Yumi—"

"And the whole time I can hear calming music, kind of like what I used to listen to when I did yoga, but now I can't anymore, because when I do, I remember that space-person thing and it makes me anxious all over again."

"Yumi, did Jean talk to you about his dreams?"

"What? No, why would he?" said Costa, looking up. "Ms. Donnelly? Why're you looking at me like that?"

"You know what? Let's go down to med bay after all," she said, gently taking Costa by the upper arm.

"Is it bad? Do I have something bad?" said Costa, her voice rising.

"No, no, I just want to check a few things. Don't worry. We're probably going to be exploring the rest of the system to see if we can find anything else promising before we go home, so I want to make sure you and the rest of the crew aren't miserable the whole time, yeah?"

"Y-Yeah. Thank you."

Although she gave Costa a thorough examination and took blood and urine samples, Donnelly couldn't find anything abnormal about her physical condition. The best she could do was give Costa the same sedatives she had given Chocaj and Wilson and hope it was all just a coincidence. However, by the time the dig was over, and the company had given Chou approval to explore the rest of the system, crew members Gupta and Iweala, geologists Micheli and Park, and one of the engineers, Meyer, had all come to Donnelly complaining of restlessness and anxiety. A few days after she saw Meyer, she brought Chou's coffee to her on the bridge as usual and explained the situation as they went through their morning protocol.

"So, are they sick?" said Chou, nursing her cup of coffee.

"Nope. No fevers, no topical changes, no internal injuries, no foreign bodies, no tumors, no infections, and no gunk in any of their organs. Everyone checks out, but they've all been saying the same thing."

"Strange. It's not like they were exposed out on that moon. We took all the necessary precautions," said Chou, her mouth quirking to the side in puzzlement. "Let's not mention this to the company for now. I'm not going to have them questioning my ability to captain the ship, and we're already making good progress with this system."

"So, what should we do about our people then? I don't have enough sedatives for everyone."

"Put in a request for their medical histories again and see if you can unearth anything. Sounds psychological. While you do that, I'll have Charlie conduct interviews with the crew."

"Charlie?" Donnelly wrinkled her nose. "No offense, Cap, but I don't think that guy should be in charge of asking people sensitive questions."

"Everyone on the ship talks to him regularly, whether they want to or not, and he's not an officer. People might be more guarded if one of us asked a personal question."

Donnelly held her tongue. She had never fought with Chou once in their entire career together, and she wasn't going to die on the hill of Charlie Vasquez.

When she begrudgingly informed Vasquez of his new duties, he insisted she be his first interviewee, but Donnelly shook him off, telling him to check the medical logs if he wanted to know what she thought. Undeterred, Vasquez did just that, then set his sights on Chocaj, Donnelly's first patient. As soon as he knocked on Chocaj's door, it slid back to reveal Halabi, who had placed her hands on each side of the door frame, blocking his entry.

"Yes?" she said.

"Hi, Kealani," said Vasquez, cracking a cheery smile. "Alexandr in?"

"Yeah, what do you want with him?"

"The captain asked me to conduct interviews with the crew. Seems people have been a bit out of sorts lately, and she just wants to make sure everyone's okay," he said in an almost condescendingly calm voice. "I'd like to talk to you too after Alexandr, if you wouldn't mind."

Halabi tapped her foot and glanced over her shoulder as she considered his proposition.

"All right, come in," she said, leading him inside.

Chocaj was in the living room, pacing about beneath the dimmed ceiling lights and biting his nails.

"Hi, Alexandr," said Vasquez.

"Oh, hi, Charlie," said Chocaj, not breaking his stride.

"Captain wanted me to talk to you about how you're feeling. Make sure you're doing okay. You mind if I record our conversation?"

"Yeah, uh, no, sure. Go ahead."

Vasquez turned to Halabi, who hadn't moved from his side.

"Could I speak with him alone? I'll let you know when we're done."

Halabi frowned but nodded and left. Once he heard the front door slide shut, he turned back to Chocaj and activated his handheld recorder.

"How're you feeling today, Alexandr?" he said, sitting down.

"Mm, not so good, Charlie." Chocaj continued walking back and forth.

"You still feeling restless?"

"Yeah."

"Worse than before?"

"Mm, yeah."

"Jasmine said she gave you some sedatives. Have they been helping at all?"

"They did, in the beginning, but the more I take them, the less effective they get."

"When did you start feeling like this?"

"Oh, God, I don't remember. Toward the end of the dig, maybe?"

"What do you think caused it? Did you see anything unusual while we were out there on that moon?"

"Unusual? Sure, but not when I'm awake."

"What do you mean?" said Vasquez, cocking his head to the side.

"I keep having these dreams," said Chocaj, shaking his head as he paced. "Almost every day since then. Just blackness and this horridly soothing music—it doesn't match at all And then this thing just stares at me. It's like a space man or something."

"Like an astronaut...?" said Vasquez, slowly.

"No, no, no, no, no, no, no, no. It's made out of space. It's not even really man shaped. It just looks like one of those chalk outlines of a dead person, you know, like at a crime scene. And it just stares at me. I try running away from it, but it keeps following me. I turn around and run, and then it appears in front of me again. I just wish it would stop."

"It's just a dream, Alexandr. It can't hurt you." Vasquez chuckled.

"Oh, shut up!"

Chocaj ground to a halt, fingers half-clenched like claws as he glared at Vasquez. A tense silence hung between them for about five seconds, then Chocaj's anger melted into apprehension, and he began pacing again.

"I'm sorry. I'm sorry, I'm so sorry, Charlie. I-I-I-I don't know what's happening. I just, I just feel like I've got to..." Chocaj dragged his hands down his face, eyes darting to and from Vasquez.

"Got to what, Alexandr? It's all right, you can tell me."

Chocaj nodded. "Sometimes... Sometimes I feel like I want to hurt someone. Or hurt myself."

"Did you ever have these sorts of thoughts before the dreams occurred?" asked Vasquez, keeping his face blank despite Chocaj's alarming statement.

"No, never, I never have," said Chocaj, then dropped his voice to a whisper. "I'm scared, Charlie."

"It's all right, I'm going to help you. Just keep taking the sedatives, and I'll see if I can convince the captain to take us home early."

"Oh, don't tell the captain, Charlie, please," Chocaj moaned. "Don't tell anyone. They'll lock me up for sure."

"All right, I promise," Vasquez lied. "Get some rest now. I apologize if I upset you. Everything will be okay."

"Wait," said Chocaj as Vasquez stood.

"Yes?"

"Do me a favor? Tell Kealani to stay the hell away from me. Tell her anything, just keep her away."

"Yeah," said Vasquez, solemn now. "Sure thing."

When he stepped out of Chocaj's room, he found Halabi waiting for him, arms crossed and puffing on a smoke pen.

"Well?" she said.

Vasquez sighed and leaned against the wall next to her.

"He's not doing so good."

"No shit."

"I can see why you're worried about him."

"Gee, is it obvious?" she drawled.

"I'm not trying to patronize you. I'm just as worried about him as you are. He's my friend too," said Vasquez, patiently.

"You're right. Sorry," said Halabi. She bit her bottom lip. "This whole thing is putting me on edge."

"Hopefully, not the same way Alexandr's on edge," said Vasquez with a wry smile.

"No, nothing that bad," she said, taking another puff.

"He told me about having some strange dreams."

"Yeah, I have no clue what he's talking about. I wish I knew. To be honest, it's scaring me."

"I think for the time being you should give Alexandr some space. We have no idea what's happening to him or any of the other crew members, and it could be contagious."

"I don't think quarantining him is going to help. It's not a disease. Jasmine's tests showed nothing."

"Space is vast. It could be something we don't know anything about. In any case, I think he would want you to keep your distance. The possibility of infecting his friends might increase his anxiety."

Halabi sighed. "Maybe you're right. I'm worried about leaving him alone, though."

"I'll discuss it with the captain. We could get him set up with a bed in med bay."

"Yeah, that might be good," mumbled Halabi. "You might wanna talk to Jean too. He's been acting up worse than Alexandr, to be honest."

With that, she capped her smoke pen and returned to Chocaj's room.

Vasquez stood a while longer in the corridor, pondering what Chocaj and Halabi had told him, then headed to Wilson's quarters. He knocked on the door, but no one answered.

He knocked again. No answer.

"Jean?" he called. Still nothing. Vasquez touched the adjacent wall panel, and instead of prompting him for an access code, the door slid open. It was dark inside.

"Jean?" he shouted from the doorway, poking his head in.

A faint light shone from the direction of the bathroom, and he could hear an indistinct tapping coming from inside. Vasquez entered the cabin slowly.

"You in there, Jean?" he said, looking around as he approached the bathroom. From what he could see from the living room, Wilson's bed was made, and his room was clean, not a single piece of dirty laundry on the floor. The slow, steady tapping from the bathroom continued.

The door was ajar.

"Jean?" said Vasquez, pushing open the bathroom door. He inhaled sharply. "Jesus Christ, what the fuck are you doing, Jean! Fuck!"

"Hi, Charlie," said Wilson, looking up with a small smile. In one hand, he held a knife. His other hand lay flat on the white bathroom counter, fingers neatly chopped into rows of thick, fleshy discs. Rivulets of blood streamed into the sink and onto the floor.

"God fucking dammit, what did you do! Shit!" cried Vasquez, pulling at his own hair in shock and confusion. "I'm getting you to med bay; we can still reattach them!"

"I don't need them." Wilson shrugged.

Vasquez grabbed the knife out of Wilson's hand and threw it into the bathtub, then seized the metal toothbrush cup next to the faucet and scooped the finger bits into it.

"Come on!" said Vasquez, pushing Wilson out of the bathroom. "Move, move!"

He dragged Wilson into the hallway amidst a mild string of protests, Wilson's serene expression not once wavering even as Vasquez hurried him through the ship, leaving a trail of crimson droplets in their wake. Vasquez punched the first communications panel they crossed, one hand clutching the cup of fingers and the other holding Wilson's sleeve.

"Captain, I have a medical emergency!" he shouted into the micro-phone. "Jean's cut off his damn fingers! I need med bay to be ready in five! Over!" Without waiting for an answer, he continued hauling Wilson along. "Fuck! Shit, man, what were you thinking?"

"Just wanted to."

"Don't give me that bullshit, man!" shouted Vasquez, his voice cracking.

"I feel better."

Donnelly was already inside the med bay when Vasquez and Wilson exploded through the doorway. She gasped.

"Oh, God, Jean! What the hell happened!"

"Didn't need them," Wilson mumbled, feebly attempting to push Vasquez off him. "Let me go. Let me go."

"Jean, you're not okay! You need to sit down," said Donnelly, rush-ing forward to help Vasquez pull him toward the examination table.

"Go away," said Wilson.

Together, Donnelly and Vasquez hoisted him onto the table and strapped his arms and legs down.

"Where are his fingers?" Donnelly panted. Vasquez held up the blood-stained toothbrush cup. Her bottom lip trembled for a second before she snatched it out of his hand and looked inside.

"Shit! What the fuck happened? I can't tell which parts belong to which fingers!"

"I walked in on him chopping up his fucking fingers like they were goddamn carrots! I didn't think! I just dumped them in!"

Donnelly shook her head and took a deep breath.

"Shit. Okay, we've got this. Come here and help me sort them," she said, handing Vasquez a pair of synthetic gloves.

"Let me go!" Wilson whined.

"Shut the fuck up, Jean!" Vasquez snapped as he dumped the finger pieces onto a sterile metal tray. "Okay... Here, this one with this one. This one... this one."

"Yeah, yeah, you've got it," nodded Donnelly next to him. "Here, this one's here."

"Fuck, my hands are shaking too much."

"It's okay. Breathe. You've got this, Charlie."

"Okay. Okay."

Somehow, they managed to get the fingers in order, and Donnelly was able to fuse and reattach them to Wilson's hand within minutes. Afterward, she injected him with a solution that would knock him out for a few hours and give his hand a chance to heal.

"He should be fine for now. I'll take care of the rest," said Donnelly, removing her gloves. Both she and Vasquez were spattered with flecks of Wilson's blood.

"I'll stay," he said, his usual bravado gone. "In case anything else happens."

"Yeah, good idea," she nodded. "Thanks."

At that moment, the med bay doors slid open, and Chou rushed in.

"What the hell is going on?" she shouted. "What happened to Wilson?"

"Charlie found him hurting himself. We have no idea why," said Donnelly. "He hasn't been making much sense. He's out for now, but I'll ask him some more questions when he—"

Before she could finish explaining Wilson's situation, a faraway yet piercing scream sliced through the ship.

"Jasmine, stay with Wilson!" Chou commanded. "Vasquez, with me!"

They sprinted toward the direction of the scream, and crew members Wong and Anderson, who had heard it as well, joined them along the way.

"There's blood!" yelped Anderson as they ran toward crew quarters.

"It's Jean's, don't worry," said Vasquez automatically, too distracted by the screaming. "Shit, that sounds like Kealani."

His theory proved correct when a moment later Halabi staggered around the corner, clutching her neck.

"Help!" she croaked, tears running down her face. "Help! He's trying to kill me!"

"What happened?" barked Chou.

"He tried to strangle me," she cried, moving her hand. Four red stripes glowed viciously on either side of her neck, scarlet half-moons crowning the far end of each stripe.

"Who?" said Chou.

Halabi sobbed. "Alexandr."

As if on cue, Chocaj appeared behind her, walking as if he were merely on his way to the cafeteria for lunch. Halabi screamed and flung herself into Chou's arms.

"No, get away!" Halabi shrieked.

"Vasquez, Anderson, restrain him and take him to med bay!" said Chou.

The four of them darted forward and seized Chocaj, though he did not resist.

"What about Jasmine and Jean?" said Vasquez.

"Tie him down somewhere away from Wilson, and have Jasmine examine him," said Chou. "Wong, take Halabi to her room and stay with her until I get back."

When they returned to the med bay, they bound Chocaj to a metal folding chair for Donnelly's examination. Vasquez and Anderson flanked Chocaj, muscles tensed and ready to spring into action in case he lashed out at her. When she finished, she pulled up another chair and sat opposite Chocaj at a safe distance.

"Alexandr?" she said, evenly.

"Yes, Jasmine?" said Chocaj, his tone light and airy, eyes soft yet cold.

"Do you know what you did just now? To Kealani?"

"I tried to strangle her, Jasmine."

"Why? Isn't she your best friend?"

"Oh, yes. She's my best friend."

"Then why?"

Chocaj smiled wistfully and locked eyes with her. "I just wanted to hurt somebody."

"Shit," Chou muttered, putting a hand to her mouth.

"Why would you want to hurt someone, Alexandr? That's not like you," Donnelly continued.

"It's like, uh, what is it? Like an itch. The space person gives it to me. The itch."

"Does the space person tell you to hurt people?"

"No. The space person never says anything. Just stands there." Chocaj closed his eyes, tilting his head upward as if communing with a god. "Always looking at me. Always playing that soothing music."

"Jasmine, Vasquez, a word outside?" said Chou, sharply. "Anderson, stay here and watch him."

Once the med bay doors closed, the three of them stood in a tight circle and lowered their voices.

"Shit, what the hell happened to them?" whispered Chou. "Wilson and Chocaj were never like this before."

"Whatever it is, it's gotta be the same thing going around," hissed Donnelly. "Yumi said she's been having the exact same dreams! The space—"

"Space person," finished Chou. "There's always a possibility they talked about it amongst themselves. Their subconscious could be associating it with whatever shared anxieties they have. Makes more sense that it being some sort of contagious disease we don't know about."

"Jean cut off his fingers, and Alexandr tried to kill Kealani, his best friend! Actual disease or not, this weird mania is dangerous. We've got to do something," said Donnelly.

"I agree," said Vasquez. "The whole ship's going to be in a panic if this gets around, and we're very, very far from home."

Chou crossed her arms and chewed on her bottom lip as she considered her options.

"Jasmine, keep monitoring Wilson and Chocaj. Get as much information out of them as you can. Vasquez, you know where the firearms are stored, right? Stay with Jasmine and make sure those two don't do anything funny. I'll have Anderson keep an eye on Costa and the others, but we'll need to be subtle about it. We don't want to make their condition worse. In the meantime, we need to keep what happened today under wraps. Like Vasquez said, we don't want widespread panic right now when we're so far from Mars, understand?"

Donnelly and Vasquez nodded, and they returned to the med bay. Chou delivered her orders to Anderson and then left to check on Wong and Halabi. She was only able to walk a few meters down the corridor before Sanjay Garcia stepped around the corner, face scrunched up in disapproval.

"Are we heading back to Mars?" he said without preamble.

"No, why would we?" said Chou without breaking her stride. Garcia followed.

"Don't play dumb with me, Annie, I heard everything."

"That's 'Captain,' Sanjay," Chou growled.

"There's been an attempted murder on this ship, and you want to keep going? For what? For a few extra credits? A big sign on that moon with your name on it?"

"Chocaj has been restrained and will be restrained for the rest of the mission. The problem has been resolved," she snapped.

"And has the problem been resolved with Jean?"

"Yes, Wilson has been restrained as well. There is nothing else that needs to be done. We are carrying on and that's that."

"If there's a sickness going around, protocol requires the ship to return to Mars for quarantine, evaluation, and treatment. You're being irresponsible, *Captain*."

"And you're being insubordinate, Sanjay," said Chou, stopping abruptly and turning to face him, eyes steely. "We've worked together for a while now, but do not think I won't confine you to your quarters if you continue questioning my authority. I know you want to go home to your family, but this is my ship, and my ship, my rules. Understand?"

"Yes, sir," Garcia said through clenched teeth.

Chou marched off, and his glare followed her until she was out of sight.

"Do they really think they can hide this from us? Everyone fucking heard Kealani screaming bloody murder," said Garcia. Stella Kidane stepped out from a shadowy nook nearby.

"Annie's just scared, Sanjay," she said. "Besides, she probably doesn't want anyone to think she's made some sort of mistake in hiring them."

Garcia scoffed. "Well, I can believe that part. All she cares about is her own reputation. You know that. You've worked with her for, what, fifteen years?"

"You're right, but she's not heartless. And right now, we need to stand by her while she sorts through whatever this mess is. Staging a mutiny isn't going to help."

"I wasn't thinking about mutiny," grumbled Garcia. "I just think she should follow protocol and turn the damn ship around."

"It's not our call," said Kidane. "Let's just be vigilant and try and make sure no one else gets hurt."

Garcia shook his head and heaved a sigh. "Fine. I trust your judgement, Stella. But could you at least tell her you think we should go home too? Maybe she'll listen if more than one person says something."

"I'll see."

That night, after everyone had gone to bed, Kidane went up to the bridge where Chou had settled in for her nightly routine, legs pulled up onto her chair and a tattered blue blanket wrapped around her as she scrolled through star charts, maps, and reports. While Kidane and Garcia usually liked to work in the lab with music playing, the bridge was silent except for the hum of the Shiro Oni.

"Hey, Stella," said Chou when Kidane stepped in. Dread, guilt, and feigned ignorance shuffled across her face. "What's up?"

Kidane pulled up a chair and leaned back into it. "Anything I can do to help?"

Chou's eyebrows shot up in confusion and surprise then drooped in resignation. "Nothing gets past you, does it, Stella?"

"I don't need to know the details if you don't want to share them. I just want to help with whatever's going on."

"That's kind of you, but I..." Chou stopped as an idea formed. "Actually, could you analyze your data from the dig? Anything you gathered from your equipment, doesn't matter how small. Try and see if you notice anything even slightly abnormal? And could you ask Sanjay to run more tests on the samples? He'll understand. We just... We're not on the best of terms right now."

"Sure."

"Thanks, Stella. You're a lifesaver," Chou sighed with relief.

"We'll see," said Kidane, and stood up. "I'll get started tonight. I don't have anything better to do."

Chou nodded and turned back to her charts.

Kidane spent several hours in the lab sifting through all the data and readings, but she found nothing to suggest anything had been wrong with the moon. They had been to dozens of planets and moons over the years, and other exploration ships had been to dozens more; there was a whole library devoted to what constituted as abnormal, and their moon had exhibited none of them. She woke Garcia before breakfast the next morning, relayed Chou's request, and followed him to the lab to assist with his analyses in the hope that he would be more successful.

Several days of testing later, Garcia threw his goggles down onto the lab table.

"Nothing. How can there be nothing?" he said, ruffling his hair in frustration. "Maybe this is something we picked up along the way before we got to the moon?"

Kidane pulled her goggles off and rubbed at the indentations left behind on her forehead. "Negative. Annie checked everything picked up by the ship from the time we left Mars until we got there."

"She sure we didn't pass through some hell dimension on the way?" said Garcia, sardonically.

"No, the ship's sensors would've picked it up," she replied. Garcia didn't bother clarifying the joke. "I'm going to go report to Annie. Do you want to come?"

"No, thanks. I need to send a transmission to my husband. It's been literal days."

When Kidane arrived on the bridge, Chou was preoccupied with watching a video Donnelly had pulled up on her portable holo-display. She looked up when Kidane entered, acknowledged her with a nod, then returned her attention to the video.

"Hello, Jean. How are you today?" said Donnelly's recorded voice.

"Not so good, Jasmine. I'm not liking these fingers," Wilson replied softly, flexing his repaired hand.

"I know, but trust me, it's for your own good. Now, Jean, do you remember what you were thinking when you cut off your fingers?"

"Just that they were tingling. People say, 'ants under the skin,' but it's not really like that. It's like the feeling you get right before a static shock."

"And you still feel like hurting yourself?"

Wilson nodded.

"Do you feel like hurting other people?"

"Either, or," Wilson shrugged. "Anything to make the restlessness go away."

"And what about your dreams? Are you still having those?"

"Yes. Now that my fingers are back."

Donnelly stopped the video. "After that, it was pretty much more of the same. Alexandr's been no different, except he smiles a lot more, the creepy bastard."

"How have the others been?" said Chou.

"Still anxious, still restless. Still dreaming."

"But you've been with them this whole time, and you haven't been feeling or seeing any of that yourself, right?"

"Other than the usual anxiety of being around a bunch of nut jobs, no. I'm perfectly fine. No space-person dreams either. What about you, Stella? You seen anything in your dreams?"

"I don't really dream," said Kidane, hands in her jumpsuit pockets.

"Typical," said Donnelly, grinning despite everything.

"Did you and Sanjay find anything, Stella?" said Chou.

"Sorry, Cap, there's nothing. We checked a hundred times."

"Damn," Chou groaned. "If it's not the moon and it's not a physical disease, then what is it?"

"It's definitely the moon," said Kidane. "That's the only logical reason. We just don't know what about the moon caused this. Could be something beyond the tools and knowledge we have."

"Well, that's just great, isn't it?" said Donnelly. "So, what? What do we do?"

Chou put her fingers together in contemplation. "...Nothing."

"Nothing?" said Kidane, a hint of incredulity breaking through her usual monotone.

"For now. We don't have enough evidence other than Wilson, Chocaj, and a lot of anxious people having the same dreams. That's not enough to base a decision off of. We'll continue exploring the system as planned and monitor the situation."

"I agree," said Donnelly. "What have we found in this system so far now? Two natural satellites with the potential for sustaining life and a couple of terraforming candidates? Those are better odds than we've had in years, and we might find something even better."

"Sanjay's not going to take lightly to that," said Kidane.

"Well, Sanjay's going to have to suck it up," said Donnelly. "If he's too short-sighted to see that what we're doing here is going to benefit his family and the rest of humanity in the long run, then that's his problem."

"Stella," said Chou, before Donnelly could spew further insults. "Please relay this plan to Sanjay and let him know that he's under orders to be discreet about what's going on with the crew."

"Yes, Cap," said Kidane, turning away slowly and leaving the bridge.

As she predicted, Garcia was furious when she told him.

"Regardless of Annie's intentions, Jasmine does have a point," said Kidane as Garcia's ears reddened.

"I don't care about her holier-than-thou bullshit. There are a billion other exploration ships that can continue where we left off!" he shouted.

"Keep it cool, Sanjay."

"I have a family, Stella. I don't have to keep cool about this. This isn't in my contract, and I'm not the type of idiot who puts their work over their family." Garcia stripped off his gloves and unrolled his sleeves.

"Where're you going?"

"To talk to Jasmine."

"You know she's even more hardheaded than Annie."

"I have to try, Stella. I have to try. She's probably in med bay by now, right?"

"Probably. Charlie'll be with her."

"Then he can hear what I have to say too."

Garcia stormed through the ship, his stomps echoing up and down the halls to the extent that Vasquez met him outside the med bay door, automatic rifle held loosely in front of him.

"Sanjay? What's up?" said Vasquez. It was less a question than a warning.

Garcia slowed and put up his hands. "Easy, Charlie, I just want to talk to Jasmine."

"About what?" said Vasquez without easing the grip on his gun.

"She and the captain want to keep on going with this exploration mission when we clearly have some very sick people on board. They need treatment. They need to go back to Mars."

"Jasmine's working with Jean right now. Come back late—"

The pitter-patter of rapidly approaching footsteps interrupted their standoff, and Halabi rounded the corner at a brisk walk, her hands clutching her stomach and her eyes downcast. When she lifted her gaze and noticed the two of them, she let out a soft yelp.

"What're you doing here?" she said to Garcia, her eyes filled with unease.

"I need to talk to Jasmine. What about you? Aren't you supposed to be resting?" said Garcia, raising his eyebrows.

"How am I supposed to rest at a time like this?" she spat. "None of you understand. You all just treat me like you'll catch what Alexandr has if you get near me."

"Of course we understand, Kealani. We're all just as freaked out as you are," said Vasquez, letting his rifle drop a fraction.

"Freaked out? I'm the one who nearly died! My own friend put his hands around my throat and tried to kill me for no goddamn reason!"

"All right, all right, calm down," said Garcia, holding his hands out.

"What illness could possibly make him do something like that to me?" she continued. "All this blather about space people and music and dreams. It's all nonsense! That's not a disease! What the fuck is it!"

"Kealani—" Vasquez began, but a scream from inside the med bay ate up the rest of his assurances.

The three of them rushed in to find Donnelly on the floor, medical tools scattered around her, chairs overturned, and Wilson on top of her, pinning her down, a scalpel raised above his head, taking aim. Without hesitating, Vasquez fired three shots, two bullets passing through Wilson's skull and the third smashing through his cheek bone, showering Donnelly with blood and bits of flesh and bone. Wilson fell to the floor beside Donnelly with a heavy thud, blood pooling beneath him. Halabi screamed.

"Charlie, what...?" cried Garcia. Vasquez lowered his gun swiftly.

"Get out, both of you," he commanded.

"Charlie—"

"I said get out!"

Garcia put an arm around the shaking, sobbing Halabi and hurried away. Vasquez waited until the door slid shut before shouldering his gun and hurrying to kneel next to Donnelly.

"Jasmine, you okay?" he asked in a low voice, putting a hand on her shoulder.

Donnelly swallowed hard, and sweat trickled down the side of her forehead, but she said nothing. She turned and scooted over to Wilson. With a trembling hand, she checked his eyes, his pulse, his skin, and his fingers. His right thumb was broken.

"He got out of the handcuffs," Donnelly whispered. "He was so fast, I didn't expect it. I didn't..."

Vasquez stood suddenly, and Donnelly watched him go over to Chocaj, who had been sitting on his bed observing the whole incident unfold with a small smile on his face. Chocaj allowed Vasquez to lay him down on the bed and secure his remaining limbs, not once taking his eyes off of Vasquez's throat.

"Thanks, Charlie," Chocaj said in a low, almost seductive voice. Vasquez shuddered and returned to Donnelly's side. She accepted his proffered arm and rose to her feet, legs still a bit wobbly.

"I need... I need to take samples," she said, her hands moving in and out of her pockets and along her thighs and stomach as if she didn't know what to do with them. "Then we... we need to... body bag. And tell the captain."

"I'll stay here while you take the samples," said Vasquez firmly. Donnelly nodded.

He stood by in silence as she extracted Wilson's blood, skin, and saliva, occasionally stepping in to help when Donnelly couldn't hold her hands steady enough. She had just finished storing vials of blood for analysis when Chou ran in, a pistol held at her side.

"What the hell happened here?" she shouted, looking from Wilson's body to Vasquez and Donnelly. "Sanjay and Halabi said you shot Wilson dead, Vasquez, so you better tell me exactly what happened right now, or there will be consequences!"

Vasquez let go of his rifle so that it hung freely across his shoulder. "Jean attacked Jasmine. He was going to kill her."

"Wasn't he handcuffed?"

"He broke his own thumb to get out and caught her by surprise. When we came in, he was just about to stab her."

"It's true," said Donnelly quietly. Both of them turned to look at her. "Charlie saved my life, Cap."

Chou studied Donnelly's face for a few seconds then put the pistol's safety back on and hastened over to her.

"Are you hurt?" she asked, putting her hands on Donnelly's shoulders. Donnelly shook her head, but when Chou tried to look into her eyes, she stared resolutely at the opposite wall. Chou pursed her lips and turned to Vasquez. "Let's get Wilson in a body bag and clean this place up. We don't need anyone else seeing this."

"We're not going to have a send-off or anything? I mean, that's Jean. That's my friend. Stella would at least want to know, as our supervisor," said Vasquez with deliberate nonaggression.

"I'll tell Stella after. She's not the sentimental type anyway. And it'll just cause even more panic if people see the body bag. We need to handle this quietly. That's an order."

Vasquez didn't protest further, possibly because he didn't have the energy to, and they hoisted Wilson into a body bag while Donnelly cleaned the blood off the floor. Despite their insistence that she should rest, Donnelly accompanied them as their lookout while they carried the body down to the airlock. None of them said any words of remembrance before Chou pressed the hatch button, and five seconds of tense, melancholy silence later, Wilson's corpse drifted into the vacuum of space.

"How is this getting around? Is this just mass hysteria?" muttered Chou as they watched the oblong figure grow distant.

"Whatever it is, we need to do something about it. Now," said Donnelly, regaining some semblance of her usual assertiveness.

"I agree, but how? We don't even know what it is. How can we possibly control it?" said Vasquez.

Chou crossed her arms tightly across her chest. "Jasmine, who else has come to you with these symptoms?"

"Costa, Micheli, Gupta, Iweala, Meyer, and Park."

"What about Kealani?" said Vasquez.

"She's shaken up after what happened with Alexandr, but she's never mentioned anything about a space person," said Donnelly. She flinched. "Shit, I forgot about her and Sanjay."

"Vasquez, go check on them," said Chou.

"No, I will. No offense, Cap, but you nearly shot Charlie's head off when you came in, and you didn't even see..." Donnelly's throat convulsed around the name. "...Jean die. I should explain things to them."

"Good point, but you shouldn't go alone. Take Vasquez with you."

"Yes, Cap." Donnelly and Vasquez nodded to each other and set off.

Chou continued watching Wilson until he was completely out of sight. Afterward, she made her way to the bridge, the slow, dull thunking of her boots devoured by the groans and rumbling growls of the Shiro Oni.

She stood in front of the bridge's communications panel for a while, hands on the control table, head down as she stared past the mechanism.

"Activate intercom," she finally said.

"Intercom activated," said the computer.

"Donnelly and Vasquez, please report to the bridge after you're finished with your duties." Chou tapped the panel, deactivating the intercom, and took her seat in the captain's chair. When the other two arrived, she swiveled around to face them, hands firmly on the armrests, shoulders back, and eyes stony with determination.

"Let me start by saying we're not aborting the exploration mission," said Chou. "As you know, this is too important to humanity for us to give up halfway, especially when we've made so much progress in such a relatively short time. That being said, I agree, we need to do something about this problem. We don't know much, but we do know that Wilson and Chocaj both had symptoms and they both worsened to the point of homicidal behavior. Therefore, to prevent further violence, I am officially ordering all crew members present-ing symptoms to be confined to their quarters until we get back to

Kuro-Ishi Station. To that end, I'm authorizing the use of weapons by those who have combat training and the establishment of a security team, led by you, Vasquez. I believe Anderson and Wong both have combat training as well. Inform them of the situation and create a shift schedule to guard and check in on the symptomatic crew members. Try to quarantine them without raising a panic. They don't need to be told everything, just get them to stay in their rooms without excessive force. Jasmine, I want you to explain the situation to whoever's left. Stella, Sanjay, and Halabi, right? And if they give you any trouble, send them my way. Now, you two have your orders. Dismissed."

"Yes, Cap," said Donnelly, but Vasquez paused.

"Captain, I agree the mission is important, but seeing as I killed someone today, how is the company going to respond?"

"I'll tell them what they need to know."

"Meaning...?"

"Asynchronous communication with company leadership is not ideal in this situation. We don't have the ability to address their concerns immediately at this distance, which may lead to impulsive decisions on their part, and I'm not going to have them making rash assumptions about our integrity nor my responsibility to my crew. Everything was done by the book, and none of them were exposed to anything on that moon. We'll figure this out and deal with it on our own, just like we've always done. Understood?"

"Yes, Captain."

"Now, go."

An hour later, to no one's surprise, Garcia marched onto the bridge, seething, with Donnelly on his tail.

"What the hell, Annie?"

"That's 'Captain,' Sanjay."

"Why the fuck haven't you turned this ship around?" he said, on the verge of outright screaming. "Furthermore, quarantining and handcuffing people to their beds when they report even the slightest bit of anxiety isn't doing much to calm people down. And what if one of them goes berserk like Jean and breaks free?"

"That's not going to happen. Vasquez and his team are patrolling round the clock. How's Halabi?"

"Awful. Don't change the subject," Garcia snapped.

"I *am* on the subject. If she starts exhibiting symptoms, she'll need to be quarantined too," said Chou, coolly.

"Leave her alone. Her best friend tried to kill her. That would mess anyone up."

"And you?"

"What about me?" Sanjay glared.

"How are *you* doing?" said Chou, pointedly. Garcia went still, like a mouse that had spotted the shadow of a hawk.

"I'm fine," he said, curtly.

"By the way, you're not to write to your husband about this."

"What're you talking about?" said Garcia, feigning innocence.

"Don't play dumb. What's happening on this ship needs to be handled discreetly. If word gets out, the company's going to be in trouble."

"Not to mention, we might lose the opportunity to mine more fuel," added Donnelly.

"Wait, are you serious? You want people to go back to that moon? The one that made everyone crazy?"

"There's no evidence that the moon had anything to do with what the crew is experiencing right now, you know that," said Chou. "We don't know what caused this, so we don't want people making assumptions, and that means we can't be telling people outside this ship about what's going on just yet."

"I'm allowed to talk to my husband," Garcia scowled.

"For the time being, you're not," said Chou. "All communications are blocked except from the bridge. Rest assured, I will report the situation to the company accordingly and they will be prepared to receive us at Kuro-Ishi under proper quarantine protocol."

Garcia's jaw dropped. "Annie—"

"'Captain.'"

"Captain," Garcia ground out. "You can't do this."

"This is my ship, and I can. We'll figure this out."

"Yeah, and how much have you figured out? Tell us, what have you found out?"

"That's enough, Sanjay," said Donnelly. "There's no point in getting riled up. Once we get home, everything will be taken care of."

"Right. Tell that to Jean."

Chou's mouth hardened into a thin line and her eye twitched.

"I'm not just fucking around here, Sanjay," she said in a low voice. "You think I wanted this to happen? I'm trying to keep calm and get everyone home as quickly as possible, and I would really appreciate it if you cooperated with me for the time being."

"So that you can keep your reputation untarnished? That's rich, putting your ego over your crew."

Chou stood, took three steps forward and slapped Garcia across the face. Almost immediately, she recoiled, pulling her hand to her chest. Garcia cradled his reddening cheek, and tears welled up in his eyes as he regarded Chou with hurt and betrayal.

"Eight years," he said quietly. "We've worked together for eight years, and this is what it's come to?"

Before Chou could answer or apologize, Garcia ran out of the room.

"I shouldn't have done that," said Chou, shaking her head.

"Probably not," said Donnelly. "But he was being insubordinate."

"This isn't going to make him any more subordinate."

"As long as he's not having space-person dreams, he's honestly low on my list of priorities," Donnelly sighed. "Like you said, everything will be taken care of once we get back, even if it means letting Sanjay go. And you're right, if people at home start spreading rumors about how we went to a moon and some people went batshit insane, people would riot. And then it's goodbye to the only major fuel source anyone has found in decades. Yes, this sucks, but we're talking about the fate of the human race, here. Sometimes sacrifices have to be made. Not that we're trying to sacrifice anyone. I mean, look at me. I was almost murdered today, but that doesn't mean I'm going to give up on this mission. I'm stronger than that. We all need to be strong for everyone on Mars."

Chou nodded, but a spark of melancholy flickered in her eyes. Donnelly put a hand on her shoulder.

"I need to get Jean's samples analyzed. You gonna be okay?"

"Yeah, m'fine," she mumbled. "Go on."

Donnelly gave her shoulder a single squeeze then briskly made her way to the med bay. When the doors opened, she stopped in her tracks. Vasquez looked up from his position about a meter or two from the prone Chocaj.

"Charlie? What're you doing here?" she said with genuine puzzlement.

"Crew quarters need patrolling, but so does med bay, especially if we get more cases like this one in here," he said, jerking his head toward Chocaj.

Donnelly nodded and approached Vasquez in a manner that tried too hard to be casual and came off as awkward. She held out a hand to him.

"Thank you. For what you did earlier. I owe you one," she muttered.

Vasquez's eyes widened, then his face settled into grim solemnity as he reached out and gripped her hand.

"No need. Anyone would've done the same," he said.

There was a moment of silence after they released each other, then Donnelly cleared her throat. "Well, I better get to analyzing Jean's samples. I doubt I'll find anything, though, since I already ran the same tests on him before."

"It's worth a try," said Vasquez, shrugging.

"Maybe you'll find the space person in there," said Chocaj from his bed. He let out a sinister chuckle that wormed its way under their skin. Vasquez adjusted his grip on his rifle, and Donnelly went to her microscope on the other side of the room.

As she predicted, by the end of the week she still couldn't find anything strange about Wilson from a physical standpoint, and Chou granted her permission to send the data without context to a doctor friend of hers on Mars to study further. Meanwhile, without any details as to why they had been confined to their rooms or why Vasquez, Anderson, and Wong regularly entered with rifles across their shoulders, the quarantined crew members' agitation continued to grow, but their persistent questions to the security team remained unanswered. Garcia and Halabi voluntarily isolated themselves in their rooms, one in protest and one to avoid interaction with other human beings, only emerging to travel to the cafeteria for meals.

Kidane took the news of Wilson's death as she did anything else: stoically and with very few words. The first thing she did was write up an incident report as his supervisor and then file it in her drafts folder for whenever Chou decided to lift the communications ban. Garcia once more attempted to persuade her to join him in confronting the captain, but she maintained her stance of solidarity, much to his profound disappointment. Resigning herself to the situation at hand, she continued reading what manuscripts she had managed to download before the communications ban and stayed out of people's way. Or at least she tried, but when Vasquez's lunch shift inevitably coincided with standard mealtimes, he would sit with her and inform her of everything going on with the quarantined crew.

"Have you talked to Sanjay at all lately?" he asked her on one such day.

"No, I don't think anyone has," she replied through a cheek full of protein goop.

"I get where he's coming from, I really do, but I also see Jasmine's point of view too, you know?"

"Mm-hm," said Kidane, sneaking a glance back down at her manuscript.

"I just wish the captain would talk to him properly, but she's just avoiding the—"

The communications device on Vasquez's belt crackled, and Anderson's voice burst from it.

"Charlie, get down to crew quarters now! Wong's—!"

The device burped static and a few unidentifiable thumps, then went silent.

"Shit," said Vasquez, and he jumped out of his seat.

"I'll go with you," said Kidane, standing swiftly.

"There's no point," he said, already in the doorway. "Not without combat training."

"You have no idea what's happened. I'm coming with you," she said, running past him.

"Dammit, boss," muttered Vasquez, and he dashed after her.

Both of them athletic types, it only took a few minutes of sprinting and careening around corners for them to arrive at crew quarters. Kidane slammed to a halt as soon as they reached the first corridor. Fresh blood was splattered across the wall opposite Wong's room and arcing red streaks had been painted on the floor by slippery boots and hands. Gupta lay on the ground, dead, his throat torn out. A limp arm protruded from the doorway to Iweala's room a little farther down. They could hear muffled voices in the distance, around the corner.

"Get behind me," whispered Vasquez, readying his gun.

The two of them hugged the wall, carefully stepping over Gupta's corpse and Iweala's arm as they went. Kidane glanced down as they passed Iweala's room. His face was purple, unseeing eyes bulging from their sockets. Drool pooled beneath his cheek, and round, purple bruises decorated his neck. She looked away.

As they neared the corner, Anderson's voice rose above the rest.

"Let her go, Wong," they heard him say above the whimpers of someone else.

Vasquez unsheathed a combat knife from his belt and handed it to Kidane. After a measured exhale, he slowly peered around the corner, finger hovering near the trigger of his gun. Kidane heard him swear under his breath and then in one smooth motion, he raised his gun, swung it around the corner, and fired two shots.

"Fuck, goddammit!" shouted Anderson when they appeared. Across from him lay a shell-shocked Costa, her pale face freckled with Wong's blood.

"No..." Costa whimpered.

"Yumi, are you okay?" said Kidane, rushing over while Vasquez checked on Anderson.

"Stay away!" Costa screamed, her expression contorting with wrinkles of terror. Kidane stopped in her tracks and tucked Vasquez's knife into the back of her pants.

"We're not going to hurt you, Yumi," said Kidane, raising her hands.

"You don't know that! No, don't come any closer!" shouted Costa. Before any of them could react, she grabbed Wong's handgun, shoved it in her mouth, and pulled the trigger. Anderson screamed as brain and pieces of skull erupted from the top of Costa's head, showering the hallway like confetti.

"Fuck!" cried Anderson. Kidane and Vasquez didn't say anything, couldn't. All they could do was stare until a harsh beep from Vasquez's communicator startled them out of their shock.

"Vasquez, what's going on down there?" came Chou's voice from the speaker. "I heard Anderson's transmission. I'm heading there right now. Talk to me. Over."

Kidane and Vasquez exchanged looks.

"Wong, uh, Wong went berserk," said Vasquez in as steady a voice as he could manage. "He's dead. Along with three others. Over."

Chou didn't respond, but she arrived a minute later, sweat soaking her face and jumpsuit. She silently took in the bloody scene, her expression unchanging except for a slight purse of her lips.

"Vasquez," she finally said.

"Yes?"

"Put everyone exhibiting symptoms in med bay and handcuff them to their beds. Twenty-four-hour surveillance."

"All of them? They'll be cramped in there. If one of them freed themselves, it'd be a massacre."

"Then make sure they don't," said Chou icily. "No one else is gonna die, understand?"

"Yes, Captain," said Vasquez, though his expression said otherwise.

"Stella, you're on guard duty now. Vasquez can train you. Jasmine and I will clean this up while you all get the rest into med bay." Chou looked around at each of them, her jaw set. "We're going home. Enough's enough."

The other three nodded solemnly. They probably would have felt more relieved by the news had they not been surrounded by the corpses of their colleagues. It took Chou and Donnelly about two hours to clean the blood and viscera off the floor and walls, put the bodies into bags, drag them down to the airlock, and send them the same way as Wilson. Meanwhile, Vasquez and Anderson rounded up the symptomatic crew members under the pretense they were evacuating crew quarters due to an "incident." The crew members had no idea what was really going on until the handcuffs clicked into place.

"What're you doing, Charlie?" said Micheli shakily, pulling lightly against the chain.

"We're just taking precautions, nothing to worry about," said Vasquez. Chocaj was in the adjacent bed, regarding Micheli intently, his fingers flexing every now and then.

"Charlie. I don't like it here."

"I know, just hang tight. You'll be out of here as soon as we get home to Mars. It'll be fine." Vasquez patted Micheli on the shoulder and left before he had to tell any more lies.

"Charlie, this is insane, we can't keep them all in there," muttered Anderson as they departed the med bay. "If they haven't gone crazy yet, they will after being trapped in there with Alexandr."

"Captain's orders," said Vasquez, looking straight ahead. "Just keep your head on straight and we'll make it back home."

"You didn't see Wong, Charlie. It was like he was a completely different person. And Yumi..."

"Like I said, keep your head on straight. Freaking out isn't gonna help you or anybody else. Just do what the captain and Jasmine say. They'll get us out of this."

"They're the ones who wanted to continue exploring the system! If we'd just gone home after we were done on the moon—"

"If we had gone home after the moon, we might not have known about all this until we were with our family and friends, and then what? Now we've got work to do, let's go."

Training Kidane proved to be quick and easy, and soon she was patrolling the med bay with the rest of them. Chou obtained permission from the company to abort the exploration mission and make emergency jumps back to Mars, though she left out some of the more graphic details from her report. Donnelly wasn't happy about canceling the mission, but she hardly had the energy to argue given she was in charge of managing both first officer and medic roles. She and Chou tried their best to push the Shiro Oni into performing more frequent jumps, but it was an old ship and overheated quickly. With each jump, they could hear the ship's creaks and groans worsening, like an old woman in the gnarly grips of arthritis.

"Dammit," said Chou as another red light lit up on her dashboard after their fourth jump that week. She sighed and put her head in her hands.

"It'll be okay, Cap," said Donnelly from beside her. "We're going to make it."

Chou didn't answer for a long moment then said in a quiet voice, "I don't know, Jasmine. This wasn't supposed to happen. How did this happen?"

"Hey, hey." Donnelly rose from her seat and knelt next to Chou. "This wasn't your fault, okay? We were doing something meaningful out here. But shit happens, and there's nothing we can do except do our best with what we're given. We got our samples from the moon, at least. That's better than we even expected."

"So many people are dead," Chou muttered. She stared at her dashboard, but her gaze was somewhere else.

"Annie."

Chou blinked and looked at Donnelly.

"It's going to be okay. I promise. I've got your back. We'll get through this together, just like we always have. Okay?"

Chou nodded and patted Donnelly's hand. "Right. Yeah."

"I've got to go down to med bay now. Are you going to be okay?"

"Yes, I'm fine," said Chou, straightening and rearranging her face into a small smile. "Thank you. Go on, I've got it from here."

Donnelly squeezed Chou's shoulder once and then left for the med bay or, as she liked to call it now, the asylum.

The med bay doors slid open, and the strains of madness enveloped her—people moaning, screaming, sobbing, wailing, and muttering to themselves. Vasquez had brought Kidane with him this time, and although it was her first day as a security officer, her face did not betray the slightest hint of emotion other than mild conviction.

"Well, I suppose Charlie's given you the rundown on what we do here," said Donnelly, snapping on her white gloves.

"Restrain them, don't let them bite you, it's okay to dislocate," said Kidane, as if reciting the answers to an exam.

"Basically. Let's start with Alexandr."

Chocaj sat on the edge of his bed, legs dangling over the side, hands loosely clasped together. His disheveled golden-brown hair was greasy, and he gave off the sour musk of someone who hadn't showered in a long time, but his gray eyes were soft and misty. He smiled at them when they came over.

Vasquez seized Chocaj's left arm with both hands, as if preparing to break it, and Kidane mirrored him. Chocaj's glassy stare roved over the three of them. His fingers twitched as he focused in on Kidane's slim neck.

Chocaj didn't struggle or say anything as Donnelly took her blood sample and examined him, which was somehow more disconcerting to Kidane than the thrashing Park.

"I don't wanna sleep! Don't make me sleep!" Park cried.

"No one's making you sleep. I just want to take a blood sample," said Donnelly.

"The space person! It's always there!" Her head snapped toward Kidane, eyes round and wide. "Have you seen it? Kidane, you've got to get me out of here. I don't wanna see it anymore."

Kidane said nothing, though her eyes betrayed a glimmer of sympathy. Micheli was no better, tears and snot pouring from his face as he pleaded with them.

"I don't belong here," he sobbed, gripping the hem of his shirt. "Please. Charlie, Kidane, you know me. You know me, I'm not crazy, please. It's just some bad dreams, I'm not crazy."

Donnelly wiped snot off his upper lip and dropped the swab into a test tube.

Once they'd finished, Vasquez stayed behind with Donnelly while Kidane headed to the cafeteria for her lunch break. About halfway there, Garcia strode out of an adjacent hallway and joined her.

"Awful in there, isn't it?" he said, grimly.

"It's not good."

"The fact that Annie hasn't told the company everything really concerns me. I mean, if they don't take the necessary precautions, who knows if this could spread back on Mars."

"I agree, but you know it's Annie's call."

"How long are we going to say it's Annie's call before things get completely out of hand?" said Garcia. "Will it still be Annie's call when all of us, including her, have gone mad? Will it still be Annie's call when we bring this back to our families?"

"Look, you're right, but this isn't a good time to be fighting with her and Jasmine. They're trying to keep things together as much as we are."

"Yeah, for the sake of those moon rocks!"

"For the sake of humanity."

"The sake of humanity? Kidane, don't you see, we're endangering humanity! Even if we don't spread anything, the company's going to get the rights to sell off bits of that moon to every nation on Mars, and then you'll have hundreds of people standing around on it, picking up who-knows-what. I don't know what was wrong with that rock that we couldn't pick up with our tech, but it's here with us now, and the fact that we don't even know how it got to the crew makes the idea of sending more people there even crazier."

Kidane said nothing, but her silence did not suggest disagreement. Garcia continued his diatribe into the cafeteria and through lunch, stopping only when Donnelly entered and glared at him.

The next morning, when Kidane awoke, the ship was quiet. The usual rumblings of the clunky old ship hadn't changed, but there was a bizarre stillness to the air that lurked in the hallways like a fog. She shouldered her rifle and proceeded toward the med bay, stepping as nimbly as she could, toe to heel. She peeked around every corner, but no one crossed her path.

When the eggshell-white doors of the med bay came into view, Kidane didn't notice anything out of the ordinary at first, but then she realized why the quiet was so terrible. No crying, no yelling, no screaming—not even a murmur from the patients inside. Kidane took the safety off her rifle and approached the doors. She punched in the code Vasquez had given her and they slid open with a hiss. Anderson stood in the doorway facing her, drenched in blood, a peaceful smile on his face. In the split second when he raised his arms to grab her throat, she could see bits of skin and hair glued to his fingers with slick, dark blood.

It was over before she could even register what happened. The weight of him pushed her to the ground, but her grip on her rifle didn't waver and the bullet passed cleanly through his chest. He stumbled, fingers brushing her neck and leaving bloody brush strokes across her dark skin as he fell. Kidane scooted backward across the floor and jumped to her feet, readying her rifle again. His breath came in labored wheezes, but he raised his head to look at her. His expression hadn't changed. Reaching out an arm covered in long thin scratches, the final remnants of his victims' desperate fight for survival, he dragged himself forward.

Kidane shook her head slowly with a mixture of pity and regret and fired again. Anderson went limp.

The med bay doors remained open, the censor still registering the presence of Anderson's feet. She knew it would be a bad idea to go inside and investigate by herself. If anyone came and saw her standing in the middle of a massacre with her still-warm rifle, she'd be shot as quickly as Anderson had.

Kidane backtracked to a nearby communications panel and called the bridge.

"Captain speaking, over," yawned Chou.

"Annie, I need you, Jasmine, and Charlie down at med bay right now," said Kidane in a quiet, low voice. "Looks like Anderson broke in and killed everyone inside. Over."

"On my way," said Chou, the last syllable cut off as she hung up.

Within five minutes, the four of them stood in the doorway, taking in the slaughter. Most of the bodies still remained handcuffed to their beds, whether splayed out across the bespattered sheets or crumpled on the floor with one arm up as if in mock greeting. The others either had their hands broken or limbs torn off entirely, after which they seemed to have tried to flee from Anderson, only to meet their gruesome end on the other side of the room, swirls and puddles of blood documenting their final struggle.

"How did this happen?" whispered Chou. No one had the answer for her.

"Your... orders? Captain?" Vasquez finally choked out. Chou looked like she wished he hadn't asked.

"We can't do this anymore," she whimpered, shaking her head, eyes still fixed on the bodies. "It's over. We can't."

"Annie," said Donnelly, grasping Chou's shoulder. "Pull it together. We're almost home. We can't give up now."

Chou brushed Donnelly's hand off. "I'm lifting the communications block. Everyone update and transmit your wills if you haven't already."

Without looking at any of them, she turned and walked swiftly down the hall and out of sight. The remaining three exchanged bewildered glances.

"What is she going to do?" said Vasquez.

"No idea," said Donnelly. "She's probably just in shock. I mean, we all are. I'll... I'll check on her, but do as she says."

"Right."

"And get this cleaned up," she continued, gesturing to the med bay interior. "I'll be back down to help once I've talked to Cap."

Donnelly dashed off after Chou and caught up with her outside the bridge.

"Annie? Annie, talk to me," she said, following Chou in. "Tell me what you're thinking."

"I'm sending an emergency transmission to Kuro-Ishi Station," said Chou, sitting at the communications console. "Code Murasaki."

"Code Murasaki... Annie, are you sure about this?"

Chou ignored her and activated the microphone. "This is Captain Annie Chou from the Shiro Oni, A-H-eight-one-five-one-seven-en-zero-six. Upon arrival at Kuro-Ishi Station, this ship must be subjected to all emergency quarantine procedures. Surviving crew members including myself should be immediately restrained and held in isolation before further analyses continue. An unknown illness has killed over half of the Shiro Oni crew—"

"Annie—"

"If all crew members have perished by the time the ship makes it to Mars, destroy the ship immediately. Source of illness is still unknown, and risk of spreading to civilian population is possible."

Donnelly reached to delete the voice message, but Chou was faster.

"Annie, what are you doing! Our fuel samples!"

"None of that matters anymore."

"Of course it matters! At least a hundred more years of fuel, remember? Fuel for humanity, Annie. We're a dying species!"

"They'll find other rocks with fuel."

"'They?' What do you mean 'they?' We're going to make it, Annie. We're going to make it. Don't you dare give up now!"

Chou stood up, and without looking at Donnelly once, walked out the bridge doors, stone-faced.

"Annie!" Donnelly shouted but didn't follow her this time. Instead, she paced around the bridge for a few minutes before heading back down to the med bay.

"Welcome back, Jasmine," said a horrible, familiar voice when the med bay doors opened. Alexandr Chocaj sat upright on his bed, leaning back on his arms, and serenely watching Vasquez and Kidane haul bodies into bags.

"He's alive?" said Donnelly, mouth agape.

"Somehow," said Vasquez, grimacing. "Seems like he was pretending to be unconscious this whole time. Anderson must've overlooked him. How's the captain?"

"She's... taking it rough. But that's natural. I mean, we all are," she mumbled.

"Did she say anything?" Kidane pressed.

"She's not in her right mind. I'll talk to her later," Donnelly replied. "Let's just get this cleaned up as quickly as possible before anyone comes by. Sanjay'll flip if he sees this, and we don't need him going to Cap and demanding she do anything stupid."

"Though," said Kidane as Donnelly grabbed a rag and began scrubbing at the blood on the floor, "Sanjay's got a point."

Donnelly's head whipped around, and her eyes narrowed. "What?"

"Jasmine, half of us are dead. You know I don't like going off feelings alone, but despite the lack of evidence, you have to admit that this all happened because of that moon. We can't send people there, and it would be safer to just dump our samples into space."

"I cannot believe I'm hearing this from you, Stella," said Donnelly, throwing the bloodied rag to the floor. "Am I the only one thinking about the future of human civilization here? Do you think I'm blind to what's been going on? Charlie and I have been with these people more than anyone, and we haven't caught anything. Neither have you, for that matter. We'll undergo quarantine procedures, and the samples will be thoroughly vetted. Cap's already told Kuro-Ishi about the entire situation. They'll be ready when we get there. We just have to keep it together and hold on for another week."

"Keep it together," Chocaj chuckled softly from his bed.

At that moment, the intercom dinged, and Chou's flat voice echoed throughout the ship. "Attention all remaining crew members. In light of recent events, I have lifted the communications block. Please be sure to update and transmit your wills in a timely fashion. I advise you all to stay locked in your cabins until we reach Mars. Quarantine protocol will be initiated upon arrival at Kuro-Ishi Station. Thank you."

Donnelly slapped a hand to her forehead. "God fuckin' dammit, Cap, what the fuck?! Charlie, go find Sanjay and do some damage control. I'm going to look for Cap. Stella, we can argue about this later, but I really need you on our side right now. Can you please just finish cleaning up in here while we calm people down?"

"All right," said Kidane, holding her hand out for Donnelly's rag.

"Thank you, Stella," said Donnelly with sincerity, and she ran out after Vasquez.

When Donnelly reached the bridge, Chou had already left. When she tried the captain's quarters, she found the door locked and the skeleton code changed.

"Annie!" shouted Donnelly, pounding on the door. "Annie, I know you're in there! Talk to me, please!"

She pleaded with Chou outside the door for ten minutes without receiving a single response before she gave up and headed back to the bridge. On the way there, she ran into Vasquez.

"How's Sanjay?" she asked.

"Bad," said Vasquez. "Kealani's dead."

"What!"

"Looks like she killed herself. I took care of the body, but Sanjay's freaking out."

"Freaking out how?"

"Not like that, but it's not good. I didn't know what else to do, so I brought him to med bay to help Stella. Thought she might be able to calm him down better than I could. Plus, it gave me a chance to take care of Kealani. How's the captain?"

"Bad," said Donnelly, shaking her head. "She's locked herself in her room, won't talk to me. I hate to say it, but it looks like we're in charge for now. Let's go to med bay and talk about this together."

"Good idea," nodded Vasquez, and they sped down the hall.

"You doing okay, Charlie?" asked Donnelly. Vasquez laughed wryly.

"I guess I could be doing worse."

"Ha! Well, I hate to say it, but I'm glad you're here."

Vasquez stared at her with no small amount of surprise, but Donnelly didn't notice.

Kidane's infectiously calm demeanor had managed to quell Garcia's anxiety, but the spell broke as soon as Donnelly and Vasquez entered the med bay and he laid eyes on them.

"Do you see what you and Annie have gotten us into, Jasmine?!" he snarled, gesturing at the row of body bags. "Their blood is on your hands!"

"That's enough, Sanjay!" said Vasquez. "Pointing fingers is not going to help."

"Nothing's going to help at this point except deleting those moon coordinates and dumping those cursed moon rocks!"

"We can talk about this later, Sanjay. Right now, we all need to calm down," said Donnelly.

"No! I've been telling you for weeks to do something about this, but you wouldn't listen! Now, we're as good as dead!"

"Sanjay, that is not helping!" Donnelly snapped.

"I'll never see my husband or daughter again," said Garcia, tears brimming. "And it's all your damn fault."

"Sanjay—" Vasquez began, but Garcia threw down his washrag and pushed past them and out the door.

"Leave him," Donnelly said to Vasquez then turned to Kidane. "I know this is scary, but we're not going to die. We're going to make it. We just need to keep a level head and stick together, trust each other, and we will get through this. Now, let's finish cleaning up and give our people a proper sendoff, then we'll talk about this like adults."

After the three of them sent the bodies out the airlock, Donnelly brought them all to the cafeteria where they sat together at one table and forced breakfast down while she repeated her pep talk.

"Do you think we should lock Sanjay in med bay?" muttered Vasquez once Kidane had left.

"He's upset, but he's not crazy," said Donnelly, fiddling with her spoon. "I think locking him up will just make him worse. Leave him for now, but let's keep an eye on him."

"I'm just worried he's going to turn Stella against us."

"A little late for that, but honestly, I'm not worried about her right now. We're almost home, there's no point in fighting. Let's just keep everyone alive until we're back on Mars."

"Roger that."

Unbeknownst to them, Kidane did not return to her room after their cafeteria meeting and instead went to Chou's room and knocked on the door.

"Annie? It's Stella."

Kidane waited for a whole minute before Chou's quiet voice drifted through the chrome slab.

"I'm starting to have the dreams, Stella," she said, sounding less like a ship's captain and more like a small child. "To be honest, I didn't one-hundred percent believe them until now. I kind of hoped that everyone was playing some awful prank on me. Or that I had mistakenly hired a cult. But it's real. I see that space person staring at me, and I know deep down that every one of those poor bastards was telling the truth. I'm scared. I don't want to go to sleep, but I can't stop myself. Even if I just take a thirty-minute nap, it's there. I know I should have Vasquez lock me up in med bay, but I feel like if I do, then there's no hope for me anymore. But maybe they'll be able to fix this when we get back to the station. Maybe I only have to hold out for a bit longer."

Kidane didn't say anything. She didn't know what to say. She wasn't even sure if she should say anything. A sob bubbled through the door.

"I want my mom."

Never before in their fifteen years of working together had Kidane seen her like this. Suddenly, the metal door felt icy under her calloused fingertips. The ship seemed to be roaring, and the fluorescent lights above her pulsed a blinding white, their tinny whine piercing her skull. Ten people were dead. Ten people were dead, and she'd done nothing.

Something slid out from under the door. A data chip.

"Emergency self-destruct codes," murmured Chou. "Just in case."

She didn't say anything after that. Placing the chip in one of her zippered pockets, Kidane left to find Garcia. He was in his cabin, but he refused to open the door to her.

"Sanjay, you don't have to open the door, just hear me out," said Kidane.

"What's the point? We're all dead. There's nothing we can do about it now," he said from the other side.

"Exactly. That's why I think we should self-destruct the ship."

A second later, the door opened and revealed a haggard but skeptical Garcia.

"What are you saying?"

"Given the rate this thing is progressing, our best option is to destroy the ship and everyone and everything on it before we reach the Ken-O Stream. It's the only way we'll guarantee this doesn't spread to the people on Mars."

"Yeah, and how're you going to get everyone to agree to that?"

"Annie was the one who gave me the codes. I'll talk to the others."

"Yeah, good luck with that. So, why're you talking to me?"

"Because I want to make sure you're okay with it. When the time comes."

The hostility drained from Garcia's face and left only a profound sadness.

"Yeah. I'm okay with it." And with that, he shut the door.

Steeling herself for the inevitable conflict, Kidane called Donnelly and Vasquez together to talk, though they insisted the discussion take place outside of the med bay, given Chocaj still needed to be guarded.

"I'll get straight to the point," said Kidane once they'd gathered. "Whatever this is, we've all been exposed, and the only knowledge we have is that it's on this ship. Neither of you will want to hear it, but I believe self-destructing the ship is the best option for the sake of the people on Mars."

Donnelly sighed and shook her head. "Did Sanjay put you up to this?"

"Not at all. It's the most logical conclusion if we're to consider the survival of our people."

"The best thing for their survival is fuel, Stella!" Donnelly snapped. "Without fuel, we're all stuck on Mars until we inevitably run out of resources and then we all die very painful deaths! Why can't you and Sanjay understand that? I feel like I'm talking to a wall here!"

"They can always send other ships to other places, even if it takes a few more months. Humanity can afford a few more months. We can't afford to bring this back to Mars."

"You're talking about suicide here, Stella! You want us all to di—" Her mouth went slack as a terrible thought crackled through her brain. "It's gotten to you too, hasn't it."

Vasquez's rifle flew up, cocked and ready in milliseconds. Kidane didn't flinch or waver, her expression unmoving as ever.

"I am perfectly sane, Jasmine. I've been considering the data and our options this entire time. None of us want to die, but if you and I are talking about the greater good here, this is it."

"Put your rifle on the ground, Stella," said Vasquez with a hint of remorse. She considered his pained expression for a moment then did as she was told. "Kick it over, please."

Kidane gently kicked it within reach of Vasquez, and he slung it over his other shoulder, his own rifle still trained on her.

"Turn around and walk into med bay," Donnelly commanded, her hands balled into fists.

"Jasmine—""Do it!"

Kidane turned and walked slowly inside, her head high. Chocaj sat up and regarded her with a curious smile.

"Rightmost bed. Now."

"Sorry, boss," muttered Vasquez as he handcuffed her to the bed farthest from Chocaj. "We'll be home soon."

Kidane didn't say anything more as they departed. There was no point.

"You finally see it too, huh?" Chocaj snickered. "The space person."

She looked down at her hands, calloused and veiny, but perfectly steady. "Yes. It's exactly as everyone said."

"Doesn't it make you itch?" he grinned. "Doesn't it make you want to just squeeze someone's neck until their eyes pop and their tongue rolls out?"

"No," she replied, making direct eye contact with Chocaj. "I don't know what it is, but I'm not afraid of it. I'll take the bastard down with me."

Chocaj didn't have a reply for her and lay back down on his bed. Vasquez came back about ten minutes later and leaned against the wall near the door, rifle held tightly. He didn't look at her, nor did he say anything, which was fine by her. She needed to think.

Vasquez couldn't stay awake forever. He would have to sleep at some point. The likelihood that Donnelly would trade with him was slim, given she was the only one left to pilot the ship. Even if he slept in the med bay, it would still give her a chance to escape. There were enough implements in the medicine cabinets that could serve as a screwdriver and allow her to escape through the vents. She would just need to ensure that Vasquez didn't wake up before she could get inside. Breaking out of the handcuffs would be easy. Wilson had done it before, after all. Her right hand would be out of commission, but luckily, she happened to be left-handed. The only problem was Chocaj. If he saw her attempt, he could possibly alert Vasquez, and it would be all over.

Deciding she needed more data to plan an effective escape, she lay down on her bed and went to sleep for the time being. The space person didn't bother her, hadn't bothered her ever since it showed up in her dreams a few days ago, and rest was more important than avoiding it. Vasquez and Donnelly were already sleep-deprived, and getting adequate REM sleep would give Kidane the advantage. They were still a few days from the Ken-O Stream. She had time.

Until the space person had come, Kidane had never dreamed, and so the blackness of her subconscious did not frighten her. Once sleep overtook her, she walked forward into the depths of her mind with no purpose other than to walk. When the music started, she didn't stop or look over her shoulder. The space person would appear before her in its own time.

The music was as vast as the darkness, like an immense chorus and yet also a single voice, but without any of the human qualities of a singer. No matter how hard she tried, she couldn't distinguish any specific instruments, even though the sounds felt familiar, like a forgotten word on the tip of her tongue. Vaguely violin, a few steps removed from a piano, perhaps something akin to what a flute would sound like through a waterfall.

The space person appeared on the horizon, or what would have been the horizon if there was one. It stood there, waiting for her, full of stars and planets. Kidane walked past it, and a few minutes later, it appeared on the horizon again, shifting slightly from side to side as if buffeted by a delicate breeze. She walked past it again, and again, and again. It never did anything to her, never interacted with her or tried to stop her, so she left it alone. All she wanted to do was walk.

She awoke to the hiss of the med bay doors opening and closing as Vasquez left, and she waited about ten minutes before sitting up. Chocaj mirrored her, rising and grinning.

"Did you see it?" he said.

"I did," she replied, studying the handcuff mechanism.

"Do you want me to help you?"

Kidane looked up. His smile remained intense as ever.

"How?" she asked. Without breaking eye contact, he snapped the bone in his thumb and slipped out of the handcuff. Hopping off the bed, he strode to the medicine cabinet, almost graceful in his deliberate, smooth movements. Reaching into one of the drawers, he pulled out a metal paper clip.

"You know how to do it?" he said, walking over to her and offering his find.

"Yeah," she said, accepting it hesitantly. "Thanks."

Chocaj watched her the entire time she picked the lock, leaning forward and holding his mangled hand behind his back. She resisted the urge to glance up and make sure he didn't try to attack her, instead focusing on performing the task at hand with as much efficiency as possible. When the cuff sprang open, Chocaj beamed with delight.

"You really are smart," he twittered. "You'll be able to blow up the ship for sure."

"You heard?" said Kidane, getting off the bed and putting some distance between them.

"Hard not to. You'll want to open the vent next, right?"

He watched Kidane go to the medicine cabinet and search through the contents until she found a pair of tweezers that could serve as an impromptu screwdriver. She then dragged a chair beneath the vent and popped the grill off as Chocaj stood behind her.

"Fantastic," he said. "But there's one thing you'll need before you go in."

Kidane turned to inquire, but before the question left her mouth, Chocaj grabbed her jumpsuit at the waist and threw her from the chair to the ground. She rolled and sprang to her feet, but Chocaj was already on her. He thrust his good hand forward and grabbed her neck with such force she stumbled backward and fell. The air rushed out of her lungs as she hit the floor, but her grip on the tweezers remained firm and she jabbed them into the side of Chocaj's neck with all her strength. He gasped and choked, but his hold on her throat didn't waver, and he smiled down at her even as blood dribbled from his neck and mouth. Kidane grit her teeth and ripped the tweezers out, blood spraying across the white floor. Chocaj immediately released her and fell to the side, gurgling and laughing through the crimson bubbles. He looked up at her with nothing less than satisfaction. Rubbing her neck and swallowing the bile threatening to spew forth, she hurried to the vent and hoisted herself inside.

She belly-crawled through the maze of tunnels in complete darkness, keeping her breathing steady and trying not to acknowledge how the walls pressed in on her. Grates along the way provided the occasional illumination, but she passed them by after only a few gulps of cool air and a cursory glance to affirm her mental map of the ship. A while later—she wasn't sure how much time had passed—Donnelly's muffled voice over the intercom reverberated throughout the ship.

"Give it up, Stella, you won't win this! Turn yourself in now and we won't hurt you! If you don't show up within the next ten minutes, we will shoot you on sight!"

Kidane kept crawling, sweat dripping off her forehead and chin, her muscles screaming. Eventually, she reached her destination: one of the crew cabins. Bunching herself up, she rotated so that her boots rested against the grate and her back was pressed against the opposite wall. It took several tries, but she finally managed to kick the grate out, though at the cost of her knees. She hissed through her teeth when she dropped to the cabin's bedroom floor, suppressing a cry of agony as pain, sharp and jagged, shot through her legs. When she wobbled into the living room to find the personal communications panel, she stopped short.

Garcia lay slumped over the desk, eyes peacefully closed as if he had just put his head down for a nap. A halo of dark blood spread across the panel beneath him, dripping onto his lap and the floor. A pocketknife lay just under his limp hand. Kidane lowered her head in a brief moment of silence before going to him and lifting him out of the chair. His now-cold blood smeared onto her chest as she carried him to the couch, taking care to position his head in a way that didn't cause the slit in his neck to gape. She folded his arms across his stomach and straightened his legs, then went to the bathroom for a towel to wipe the blood from the communications panel, making sure to stash the pocketknife in her boot.

"New transmission to Kuro-Ishi Station. Babylon, Mars, R-six-zero-zero-seven-three-eight-two-nine-three-two-three," she said quietly.

"Recording," said the computer.

"This is Stella Kidane, Chief Engineer of the Shiro Oni. Everyone's dead except me, Captain Annie Chou, First Officer Jasmine Donnelly, and Charlie Vasquez due to an unknown, contagious illness we picked up from the dig moon. I will try to self-destruct the ship with codes given to me by Captain Chou, but if that doesn't work, destroy the Shiro Oni on sight. If you receive this transmission after the ship has entered the Ken-O Stream, do not let anyone or anything off the ship, including myself, no matter what anyone says. Consider this entire ship a threat to the human race. End recording."

"Recording complete."

"Send transmission."

"Transmission sent."

She stood and made for the vent in the bedroom when suddenly the intercom blared.

"Annie, what are you doing!" shouted Donnelly. "Stop! Don't! Charlie, get down to the airlock and stop her!"

Kidane's stomach lurched. Instinct told her to run and save Chou from blowing herself out the airlock, but she knew it was pointless, and if Vasquez was preoccupied, then this was the perfect opportunity to make a run for the bridge.

Ignoring the pain in her knees, Kidane sprinted out of the crew quarters. If Donnelly was still watching the ship's security cameras, she would see Kidane, but she would have to decide whether saving Chou or defending the bridge was more important, and by the time she did, Kidane would be there already.

To her relief, the bridge was empty when she arrived. Sitting in the captain's chair, she activated the security cameras and put their holo-display off to one side as she put the self-destruct data chip into the computer. Down in the airlock, Vasquez and Donnelly were at a standoff with Chou, who had gotten her hands on a rifle from the armory. Donnelly was shouting something, gesticulating desperately. The computer dinged, acknowledging the presence of the chip, and Kidane tore her gaze away from the scene playing out on the cameras to run the self-destruct protocol. The process was, unsurprisingly, long and convoluted, and she barely had time to glance up at the camera feed and watch Vasquez shield Donnelly from a string of bullets fired by Chou, or witness the former captain activate the airlock doors while Donnelly stumbled out of the room, dragging Vasquez's body along with her, just in time before Chou was sucked out into space with an eerie look of calm on her face.

By the time the self-destruct countdown began, Donnelly stood in the doorway to the bridge, face stained with blood and tears, rifle held tightly in hands that shook with either terror, grief, rage, or perhaps all three.

"Get. Out. Of Annie's chair," she said, hoarsely.

Kidane rose slowly but kept herself between Donnelly and the dashboard. "Is Charlie dead?"

"You shut your damn mouth!" Donnelly spat. Her lip quivered. "I know you're not in your right mind, Stella, but how could you? We're so close to home."

"I am in my right mind, Jasmine, that hasn't changed. This is what Annie wanted too, that's why she gave me the codes."

"No! You have no idea what Annie wanted! She would've told me something like that! Before today, she was... She was..." Fresh tears splashed onto the black gunmetal. "We're so damn close. I can't give up. I can't. Not now."

In her anguish, the barrel of the rifle lowered a fraction, and Kidane dove to the side. Donnelly fired but missed as Kidane zig-zagged toward her, catching the barrel in one hand and forcing it up. Her ears rang as bullets whizzed by her head and peppered the ceiling. Something burst above them, triggering the ship's alarm. Sirens blared and the lights pulsed red as they wrestled for the gun. Although Kidane had more muscle, more training, Donnelly's eyes blazed with an overwhelming despair, and with a roar, she reeled back and punched Kidane in the face. Fireworks erupted in front of her eyes, and she heard her nose snap, felt her teeth bounce onto her tongue. Then, a singular deafening crack as something hot lodged itself in her stomach. Vision returning, she looked down and watched the spreading dampness on the front of her jumpsuit.

"I'm sorry, Stella," Donnelly whispered and then crossed to the control panel.

As Donnelly began the process of aborting the self-destruct sequence, Kidane removed the pocketknife from her boot and charged. Donnelly turned around, raising her gun, but it was too late. The blade sunk into her chest to the hilt, piercing her heart. Kidane caught her as she fell, lowering her gently to the ground as the light faded from Donnelly's eyes. Putting her forehead against Donnelly's, Kidane squeezed her hand once and then heaved herself into the captain's chair. She tapped on the panel to restart the self-destruct program, but the computer only beeped at her. The display flashed an error message stating only authorized personnel could access the captain's computer via voice activation. Donnelly had locked her out.

Her jumpsuit was soaked with blood now. She could feel it traveling down her legs. The bullet inside her had certainly hit something vital, though whether she died from organ failure or blood loss, it wouldn't matter in the end. She had pushed her body this far, but soon not even sheer willpower would be able to keep her going.

With what strength she had left, Kidane limped over to the communications panel. She spit out the blood flooding her mouth and forced down a gulp of air.

"New transmission to Kuro-Ishi Station. Babylon, Mars, R-six-zero-zero-seven-three-eight-two-nine-three-two-three."

"Recording."

"This is Stella Kidane, last surviving crew member of the Shiro Oni. When attempting to destroy the ship, I was attacked by Jasmine Donnelly. I took her life in self-defense but sustained fatal injuries. Donnelly locked me out of the ship's systems, and I am unable to restart the self-destruct program or redirect the ship. Therefore, I implore you to deploy military units to destroy the ship as soon as you receive this transmission. Destroy it or put yourself at risk of a disease that I cannot say we'll ever fully understand or control. Destroy this ship and never go to that moon. No cargo and no coordinates are valuable enough to put humankind at risk. Destroy this ship immediately. This is my last and only request. End recording."

"Recording complete."

"Send transmission."

"Transmission sent."

Kidane fell back into the chair, her energy spent. She would've liked to get a better view of the universe from the captain's chair in her last moments, but after a long career in engineering, she had come to accept the fact that sometimes things didn't always work out the way she wanted them to. And it wasn't a bad view from the communications panel.

As she felt her lungs struggling to expand, she wondered what she could have done differently. What would have been a better procedure? What would the results have looked like if she had acted earlier or more aggressively? If she wrote a manuscript about the entire event, what would she say? But as her brain lost oxygen, the science and the data dissolved into serene nothingness, and the only thing left to keep her company was the space person, swaying and staring at her while the music washed everything else away.

Acknowledgements

I would first like to thank Timber Ghost Press and C.R. Langille for giving this story a happy home and giving me the opportunity to share it with the world. Many thanks as well to editor Beverly Bernard, and to Wes Greaves for crafting the gorgeous cover art. I would also like to thank my HWA mentor, Eric J. Guignard, for his invaluable guidance and insight, and my beta reader Camilla Tejada, who whipped this story into shape and brought it to where it needed to be. Lastly, thank you to my friends and family who enabled me to be here. Without you, this story wouldn't exist.

About the Author

Catherine Kuo (she/her) is an Asian American writer who currently resides in Arlington, Virginia. Her short stories can be found in the "Bloodless" anthology, published by Sliced Up Press; the "Monstrous Futures" anthology, published by Dark Matter Ink; and the charity anthology "Dark Corners of the Old Dominion," published by Death Knell Press. She can be found on Twitter at catherinekuo531.

A Note from Timber Ghost Press

If you enjoyed *The Space Person*, please consider leaving a review on Amazon or Goodreads. Reviews help the authors and the press.

If you go to www.timberghostpress.com you can sign up for our newsletter so you can stay up-to-date on all our upcoming titles, plus you'll get informed of new horror flash fiction and poetry featured on our site monthly.

Take care and thanks for reading *The Space Person!*

-Timber Ghost Press